S is for Snowman
God's Wintertime Alphabet

By Kathy-jo Wargin

Illustrated by Richard Johnson

ZONDERk·dz

ZONDERVAN.com/
AUTHORTRACKER
follow your favorite authors

A is for Angels

White snowy **A**ngels with wide sweeping wings—
let's find the wonders that God's winter brings.

B is for Birds

Winter brings **B**irds busy searching for seed.
We'll fill the feeders to give what they need.

C is for Cookies

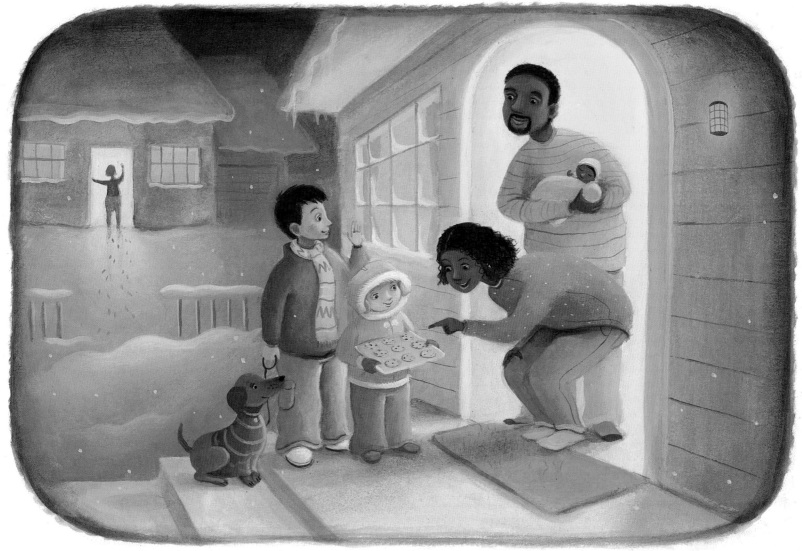

We can bake Cookies to eat and to share
and bring them to neighbors to show that we care.

D is for Decorations

Let's make **D**ecorations to hang on the tree.
Place the star at the top so it's easy to see.

E is for Evergreen

The **E**vergreen branches
will twinkle with light
to tell us God's love is
eternally bright.

Fis for Frost

God casts the Frost sparkling white on the land,
a beautiful blanket spread right from his hand.

G is for Gifts

It's time to share **G**ifts! God helps us believe
that **G**ifts are much better to give than receive.

Would you like **H**ot chocolate?
It's tasty and sweet.
Let's add the marshmallows—
Oh! What a treat.

H is for Hot chocolate

I is for Ice Skating

Winter means **I**ce skating; we love the sound of our skates on the ice as we all spin around.

J is for Jingle bells

Jingle bells Jingle! The whole
world enjoys
the sound of bright bells as they
make joyful noise!

K is for Kind

In winter, be **K**ind, doing chores great and small,
for we are God's workers and he loves us all!

L is for Lights

Winter means windows with Lights shining through.
Each candle reminds us that God's love is true.

M is for Mittens

Let's find our **M**ittens—we each have a pair,
and if we have extras we're happy to share!

N is for North wind

The **N**orth wind brings chills to our heads and our toes.
It sends the snow drifting wherever it blows.

O is for Overcoat

Put on your **O**vercoat—no time to fuss!
Warm coats are reminders that God protects us.

P is for Prayer

When walking outside in the cold icy air,
the silence of winter is perfect for Prayer.

Q is for Quilt

A **Q**uilt on our laps as we sit down to rest,
each square tells a story of how we are blessed.

R is for Ride

It's time for a Ride on a
long wooden sled.
We race the others—now look
who's ahead!

S is for Snowman

Let's build a **S**nowman with eyes made of coal.
A top hat and scarf warm his jolly old soul!

T is for Trees

The Trees are all covered in snow pure and white,
a symbol of God's purest love and delight.

U is for Universe

In winter the **U**niverse calls us to play,
as beautiful nature surrounds us each day.

V is for Visit

A good time to **V**isit our friends young and old
and bring them hot soup when the weather is cold.

W is for Wonder

For winter brings **W**onder in things great and small,
and we must remember that God makes it all!

X is for eXtra-warm

The e**X**tra-warm blankets are stacked in a pile,
so let's go inside to warm up for a while.

Y is for Yarn

Knitting with Yarn as we sit side by side,
we look out the window and watch others slide.

Z is for Zoom

Zoom! goes a sled as it speeds down the hill.
God's love is warmth for a winter's day chill.

From mittens to snowmen and angels with wings—
may your hearts know the wonders that God's winter brings.

To Jake and Ed, for the warmth and laughter you bring to every season.

K.W.

ZONDERKIDZ

S Is for Snowman
Copyright © 2011 by Kathy-jo Wargin
Illustrations copyright © 2011 by Richard G. Johnson

Requests for information should be addressed to:
Zonderkidz, 5300 Patterson Ave SE, Grand Rapids, Michigan 49530

ISBN: 978-0-310-74077-3 (softcover)

For Sushila

Love, Richard

Library of Congress Cataloging-in-Publication Data

Wargin, Kathy-jo.

    S is for snowman / written by Kathy-jo Wargin.
    p. cm.
    Summary: Presents rhyming sentences for each letter of the alphabet that remind the reader of God's blessings in winter.
    ISBN 978-0-310-71661-7 (hardcover)
    [1. Stories in rhyme. 2. Winter—Fiction. 3. God—Fiction. 4. Alphabet.] I. Title.
PZ8.3.W2172Saai 2011
[E]—dc22
    2009037507

Editor: Barbara Herndon
Art direction: Jody Langley

Printed in China

13 14 15 16 17 18 /DSC/ 10 9 8 7 6 5 4 3 2 1